Detachment from Attachment

Detachment from Attachment

Gift of Freedom from Suffering

By **Sirshree** Tejparkhi

Copyright © Tejgyan Global Foundation
All Rights Reserved 2017

Tejgyan Global Foundation is a charitable organization
with its headquarters in Pune, India.

ISBN: 978-81-8415-639-3

Published by WOW Publishings Pvt. Ltd., India

First edition published in May 2017
Second reprint in November 2019

Copyrights are reserved with Tejgyan Global Foundation and publishing rights are vested exclusively with WOW Publishings Pvt. Ltd. This book is sold subject to the condition that it shall not by way of trade or otherwise, be lent, resold, hired out, or otherwise circulated without the publisher's prior written consent in any form of binding or cover other than that in which it is published and without a similar condition including this condition being imposed on the subsequent purchaser and without limiting the rights under copyright reserved above, no part of this publication may be reproduced, stored in or introduced into a retrieval system, or transmitted, in any form, or by any means, electronic, mechanical, photocopying, recording or otherwise, without the prior written permission of both the copyright owner and the above-mentioned publisher of this book. Any person who does any unauthorized act in relation to this publication may be liable to criminal prosecution and civil claims for damages.

Although the author and publisher have made every effort to ensure accuracy of content in this book, they hereby disclaim any liability to any party for any loss, damage, or disruption caused by errors or omissions, resulting from negligence, accident, or any other cause. Readers are advised to take full responsibility to exercise discretion in understanding and applying the content of this book.

Contents

Preface: Mind and Attachment   v

1. Why Detachment from Attachment   1
2. What Can Help in Detachment   7
3. Attachment to Objects   13
4. Attachment to Wealth   16
5. Attachment to People   21
6. Attachment to Problems and Events   24
7. Attachment to Thoughts   31
8. Balancing Head and Heart for Detachment   37
9. Attachment to Fruit of Actions   40
10. Attachment to the Body   48
11. Who Can Help in Detachment   54
12. How to Develop Detachment   56

Preface

Mind and Attachment

The demon king Ravana had ten terrifying heads. What do you think they signify? They represent the ten dreadful facets of the mind: anger, ego, fear, greed, comparison, boredom, hatred, envy, attachment, and lust. Among these the five major ones are anger, greed, lust, attachment, and ego. These defilements form the main chain that binds us to suffering by making us forget our intrinsic blissful nature. The mind exists because of these defilements or vices. It can also be said that because these vices exist, the mind exists.

The mind is basically unsteady and constantly fluctuating with continuous changes occurring in it. If in the morning the mind is filled with anger, then it is filled with jealousy in the afternoon, greed in the evening, and confusion at night. Every moment it is changing. Sometimes it is sad and sometimes happy. One moment it is filled with trust and the next moment it is full of distrust and suspicion. For a moment it is very sincere and the next moment it is filled with deceit. There is compassion one moment that changes to anger the next moment. One moment it was ready to die for someone, and the next moment it jumps up to kill the same person.

Does such a wavering mind deserve to be trusted? Unfortunately, we have become attached to this ever changing mind. We have in fact become one with it and we feel *we are the mind*. We have developed faith and reverence for this erratic and fickle mind.

The truth is *the mind is an illusion.* This means it does not exist but only appears to exist. How does this happen? It is just like a straight wooden stick which when immersed in water looks bent, but is actually not. It is like a rope that looks like a snake in the dark, but is actually not. It is only because of darkness that a rope appears to be a snake. Likewise, it is only due to spiritual ignorance that the mind seems to exist, but it actually does not. To know the mind, it is necessary to look at it under the light of wisdom.

The mind gets created because we become identified with it. The moment we say, "*I am the mind,*" the mind gets formed. As soon as we get associated with the mind, we become the mind and feel *I am the mind.* When we get associated with wealth, we say *I am wealthy.* When associated to position, we say, *I am the manager/ the boss.* When associated to religion, we say, *I am a Hindu/ Muslim/ Christian,* etc. You become that to which you add an 'I'.

For example, during a marriage ceremony the bride garlands the groom or puts a ring on his finger. Just a moment earlier, no one from the other side was a relative nor did she have any attachment to anyone. As soon as she puts the garland or the ring on the groom, so many relations get established such as mother-in-law, father-in-law, brother-in-law, sister-in-law, and so on. With this long line of relatives begins the game of attachment. In the same way, when you feel, 'I am the mind,' i.e. when you garland the mind, all the relatives of the mind become your relatives. This too is a long list—anger, lust, hatred, envy, competition, confusion, hopelessness, fear, sorrow, excitement, friendliness, enmity, restlessness, success, failure…—and you get related to all these relatives.

Desires (longings or wants) are the biggest weapon of the mind. The mind derives its life from them and also sustains due to them. Therefore, the main job of the mind is to keep the desires and wants alive. It constantly arouses desires, and the desires continue to increase all the time. When these desires do not get fulfilled, you feel angry. When desires get fulfilled, it leads to greed. With greed, you begin to acquire more and more objects, and then you start getting attached to those objects. When you have accumulated a sizeable quantity, you start becoming egoistic.

In this manner, the chain of bondage is connected together by various links. However, any chain is as strong as the weakest link. If you weaken the link of 'attachment' by attaining and applying spiritual wisdom, the chain can be broken. The opposite of attachment is detachment, indifference, unconcern, or apathy. The moment you become indifferent, how can the chain of bondage remain intact? This book intends to break this weak link. We have to live in this world with detachment, just like the lotus that remains detached and pristine despite the swamp and the dirt surrounding it. The ensuing chapters will help you to break this weak link by getting rid of attachment and attain freedom from suffering.

1

Why Detachment from Attachment

There are two kinds of people in this world. The first kind are those who are dependent on other people and objects for their happiness, while the second kind are those who are not. Most people belong to the first category, while very few belong to the second.

When a girl wins the Miss Universe contest, a crown is placed on her head. This crown belongs to her for the period of one year only. But if she starts getting attached to this crown or this title, then she will remain unhappy throughout her life after she has to give it up. This means that the biggest cause of sorrow is 'attachment'.

Attachment means longing, fondness, craving, or obsession. If you are liberated from attachment, you are liberated from sorrow. And liberation from sorrow means merging with bliss.

So, does your happiness depend on someone else? Are you a slave to someone else? Or is your bliss with you?

The supreme truth is that we are the formless, limitless, divine Self or Consciousness. Bliss is our intrinsic nature. We don't need to depend on anyone else for it. But since we have forgotten this truth, we think of ourselves as limited individuals. We search for happiness outside of us and become dependent on others. If a wife is totally dependent on her husband or the husband on his wife, each one ends up in servitude to the other. We become a slave of comforts and consequently of other people, thinking that if we do not serve these people, they will not provide all those comforts.

> Once Emperor Akbar, while having his lunch, praised a pumpkin dish that was served. His advisor Birbal also started extolling the virtues of pumpkin. Next day, when another dish of pumpkin was served, Emperor Akbar was happy and praised it again. And Birbal too gave an account of numerous benefits of this vegetable. When on the third day yet another dish of pumpkin was served, Akbar was furious. "Why is pumpkin being served every day? It's terrible." Birbal agreed. "Yes, my lord. There is no vegetable worse than pumpkin. It has so many negative characteristics…" And he went on to explain all the problems caused by it. Emperor Akbar was taken aback. "Till yesterday you were singing praises of pumpkin and today you are speaking ill about it. That means you have been untruthful. Why are you doing this?" Birbal humbly replied, "My Lord! I am *your* slave and not of the pumpkin."

When one becomes a slave of another, he puts up with that other person throughout his life and keeps agreeing with everything that person says. He spends his entire life blinded and bound by attachment. Due to greed, he is unable to forgo wealth, position, or any of the comforts that he receives from others and hence lives a life of slavery. Living happily with minimum comforts is true growth and progress. Due to attachment to material comforts, he becomes a slave of other people. The one who can exercise discipline over one's body, will not become a slave, but will live a desire-free supreme life.

Supreme desire-free life means that which is beyond attachment and aversion. When attachment is conquered, supreme desire-free life begins. If we get attached to status, power, wealth, objects, gains, and luxuries, it gives rise to ego. "My position, my house, my name, my work is more important and better than others" becomes our delusion. This delusion gets converted into attachment. Attachment makes us a slave and may also push us into wrong actions. Let us therefore not become a slave of attachment, but strive to attain freedom from it if we want to live a happy life.

Love or Attachment?

There is another important aspect of attachment. When we become attached to someone, we don't even realize how and when it happened. Attachment hides under the guise of love and creates an invisible bondage. Many people are able to give up many of their wrong tendencies and habits, but they cannot free themselves totally due to this bondage of attachment.

Take a look at your life to check when do you get stuck in attachment? You may feel it's love, not attachment. But you have to understand if it's really love or attachment. In the name of love, people get entangled in desires and attachment. They may not even know the meaning of true love but they always speak of love and think that their actions arise from love. Attachment is a subtle vice of the mind; in fact, it is so subtle that we don't even feel it's a vice.

Thus, most of us do not believe attachment to be bad, because it is usually enveloped in the cloak of love. A mother loves her child but does not even realize when love turns into attachment. For instance, when her child falls sick, tears well up in her eyes. When the child does not eat, she too stops eating. If the child does not sleep, she also remains awake. This kind of fixation is attachment. She fails to realize that by remaining hungry or sleepless, she is not helping her child. If she is healthy, she can take good care of her child. But due to attachment, she thinks that it would be wrong if she eats while the child cannot. This is how love becomes attachment.

We believe that if we love someone or something, we should have attachment for it. This is a totally wrong belief. Attachment does not help us in any way. In fact, it is always harmful and leads to pain and suffering. Hence, let us cultivate love but develop detachment from attachment in order to lead a blissful life.

Attachment and Anger

Anger is also connected to attachment. In fact, anger does not arise without some form of attachment or obsession. But people often believe anger to be bad and attachment to be good. However, there is a deep relation between the two. They may look different but are actually two sides of the same coin. It is not possible to keep one side of the coin and get rid of the other. People want to be free from anger, but are not ready to relinquish attachment. This is because attachment is covered by love, while anger is covered by hatred. Anger may rankle and bite while attachment may feel good, but it is essential to be free from both, since both have the same shelf life.

> An old lady went to a doctor and complained of pain in her right knee. The doctor prescribed her some medicines. The lady inquired about the cause of the pain. The doctor said it's due to old age. The lady asked, "But why there's pain only in the right knee, when both the knees are of the same age?"

Likewise, anger and attachment are of the same age. As long as there is attachment, anger will arise due to some reason or the other. When attachment ceases, anger will also cease. However, both do not trouble you equally. Only anger bothers and troubles you. The same is not felt about attachment. Attachment enchants you and wraps you under its spell.

Attachment and Desires

It is also due to attachment that you have wants, wishes, and desires. Just as liberation from anger and attachment is essential, freedom from desires is equally important. If there is attachment, there are desires. If there is no attachment, there are no desires. And if there are no desires, the possibility of anger reduces progressively. For instance, if someone is watching his favorite show on television, then there is a subtle desire in his mind that there should not be a power failure. And if a power failure occurs at that time, then it is but natural that he feels angry. We are not able to detect such subtle desires. This is an example of a subtle desire becoming an attachment. We need to achieve freedom from all subtle as well as overt, minor as well as major desires, in order to lead a happy life.

It is also important to realize that our attachment does not stop with desires, people, wealth, objects, or status. It extends to our profession, our religion, ideologies, and our country. Furthermore, we get attached to events, to our past and future, to our thoughts, ideas, emotions, actions, our image, and to our body as well. In the chapters that follow we will learn how these attachments cause suffering and how we can detach from them in order to experience true freedom and joy. In the process, you will discover your true self—which is already liberated! So, let us begin this marvelous journey of reaching beyond attachment and detachment.

2

What Can Help in Detachment

Everyone is deeply attached to some form of attachment. So, how will you give up attachment? You will be ready to give it up only when you realize that attachment is not a gem, rather it's grime or dirt. If you believe attachment to be a precious gem, you will take great care of it and keep polishing and holding on to it. In the dazzle of attachment, we become blind. One blind man guides another blind man into the muddle of attachment and everyone is caught in its web.

The true nature of attachment will be visible in the light of spiritual wisdom. You will be clearly able to see that attachment is like grime or dirt and then it would be very easy to give it up. When dirt sticks to your hands, you rush to the tap to clean it up at once. When there is filth on your body, you rush to take a shower as soon as possible. Why do you do that? That's because you care for your health and you want to avoid any infections. Similarly, the sludge of attachment affects your overall health and happiness. It is an obstacle in the attainment of permanent happiness; it causes sorrow and suffering. Most importantly, it prevents you from achieving your ultimate purpose of coming to Earth. Hence, it is crucial not to be blinded by the dazzle of attachment, but to see it with clarity. As soon as attachment is brought to light, you discover its reality and become free from a life of servitude and dependency.

When we sweep the floor in our house, we collect all the rubbish and throw it into the dustbin. We do not call this activity as 'sacrifice'. We also do not keep count of how much of it we have thrown away. That's because we know it's trash and hence there is no question of calling it a sacrifice. It can be called a sacrifice or 'giving up' only when something precious is given away. Throwing away garbage is not sacrifice but merely common sense. If you can treat attachment and longing in the same way, it will not be difficult to give it up and get liberated from it.

Purpose of Your Life on Earth

When we are tied down by attachments, we live an unconscious mechanical life. We forget the ultimate purpose of our life. In the epic *Ramayana*, when Laxmana falls under the spell cast by Indrajit, he becomes unconscious and slips away from his goal, when he was quite close to it. In the same way, despite being close to our goal of supreme bliss (which is right within us), we remain unconscious of it because of the effect of attachment. A potent remedy or rather a panacea (*Sanjivani*) becomes necessary to break this spell of unconsciousness. This panacea will break our unconsciousness and raise our level of awareness.

So, what is this panacea? It is knowing and attaining the ultimate purpose for which we have come to Earth. When Hanuman on the command of Lord Rama brought the Sanjivani, which was given to Laxmana, the spell broke and Laxmana woke up to attain his goal. Likewise, if we can attain spiritual wisdom from our guru and attain our ultimate goal, we can also be liberated from the spell of attachment.

So, what is our ultimate goal? What is the whole and sole purpose of our life? It is discovering the answers to the most important questions: Why have we come to Earth and where have we come from? What are we going to learn, understand, and attain before we return? Until we attain this ultimate goal, the spell of attachment is not going to break. If we get stuck in small things and then leave this world lost in illusion and attachment, it would be too late by then. Let us understand this crucial matter with the help of a story.

> Suppose you are living with a mischievous boy in a 'Bright Palace'. This boy keeps throwing things around and breaking everything. You are extremely worried about it. That is why you decide to take this boy to a school for appropriate training. This school has a special method of training children. You arrive in the school with the boy in tow. You decide to take him around and inspect the school before getting him enrolled. The boy is introduced to the other students in the school. You tell him that these people will become his mother, father, brother, sister, uncle, and so forth. The boy begins to enjoy the atmosphere and starts playing with his new relatives.
>
> Meanwhile, instead of getting the boy enrolled, you go and

lie down on a bench under a tree in the school garden. You fall asleep with the soft breeze blowing across the lawn and start dreaming. The boy in the meantime due to his old habit starts fighting with those people. And then due to attachment to his home, the boy insists on returning home before the training could begin. You wake up from your sleep and your dream, and repent upon having wasted so much time believing the dream to be a reality and getting stuck in it. If during that period, you had enrolled the boy in the school and met the principal for remedying the tendencies of the boy, this situation would not have arisen. As you unwillingly take the boy back, you start thinking about what he would do in the Bright Palace. He would break things as usual!

In this analogy, the boy represents your mind, for the training of which you have come to Earth. The habits of the mind are ego, hatred, loathing, ill-will, and the like. Due to ego, the boy gets angry. Due to anger, he destroys the Bright Palace. The school is this Earth where training is imparted to the boy to make him fit for living in the Bright Palace, so that he can attain the ultimate purpose of life. Under this training, the mind is taught how to get rid of attachment with objects, people, thoughts, and the body. To teach this art, some pretend relatives are also provided.

The aim of this game is to purify the mind of all tendencies and vices, to make it unwavering, obedient, pure, and loving, so that it becomes eligible for living in the Bright Palace (attaining eternal bliss). But you have fallen asleep in the school's garden, i.e. you are living an unconscious life caught in the illusion of this world. Absorbed in your dreams and thoughts, you have forgotten your ultimate purpose of coming to Earth. When it was time for you to leave the world, you woke up and painfully realized your mistake—that you neither arranged for training your mind nor did you meet the principal or Guru.

If you had met the Guru for training the mind, you would have come to know about all the rules of this school (life on Earth). You may have received valuable advice. The secret of how not to fall asleep in this garden of illusion might have been taught to you and the boy may have got well trained and much improved. He could have even become the Prince of the Bright Palace.

From the above analogy, you may have understood why you have been provided with kith and kin, and why you should not get stuck in attachment to them, or rather to anyone or anything in this world. The most important learning is to always remember the actual purpose of your life on Earth, so that your visit to this world is not wasted. With this potent remedy of wisdom, you will never fall unconscious under the spell of this worldly illusion, and the weapon of attachment will be unable to cause any damage to you. Sorrow will always be defeated and bliss will forever be with you.

Besides wisdom, devotion for God will also help you in developing detachment. Your love for God or Supreme Self will gradually go on liberating you from the web of this illusory material world.

In fact, it can be said that wisdom helps you to attain liberation and devotion facilitates in getting permanently established in liberation.

This is because devotion plays a major role in relinquishing your ego and surrendering the mind. Thus, wisdom and devotion together are essential to attain freedom from attachment and suffering.

In the following chapters, we will learn about various specific attachments and how to detach from them.

3

Attachment to Objects

Attachment is born when we feel that we own something. We assert our ownership over objects, houses, our children, and so forth. And when something happens to any of these, it leads to sorrow. For instance, if "my watch" breaks or "my cell phone" is lost, *I* feel very unhappy, but if the same happens with someone else, it affects me only to some extent or not at all. Similarly, we find deep attachment to "my house," "my money," "my car," "my jewelry," "my clothes," and so on. Whenever the word "my" is added to any object, it gives birth to attachment and consequent suffering. To be free from such attachment, first let us bring it to light. Then the sense of ownership needs to be eliminated, at least within your mind.

This can be done by living like a guest in this world. When you live like a guest, you won't get attached to any of these things. Therefore, remind yourself each day that you are a guest in this world, and a guest does not claim ownership over anything in the house. He uses everything available in the house but does not get attached to them. A little story will make this clear.

A monk came and stood in front of a mansion at midnight, and started shouting, "Is there anybody inside?" The security guards rushed out and asked him why he was shouting. The monk told them that he wanted to spend the night in this guesthouse. The guards informed him that this is not a guesthouse but the palace of the King. The monk refused to accept and insisted on going inside.

Hearing the commotion, the King came down. When he listened to what the monk had to say, the King asked him the reason why he felt that his palace is a guesthouse? In turn, the monk asked the King, "Who was staying here before you?" The King said it was his father. The monk then asked, "Who was staying here before him?" The King replied that it was his grandfather. The monk said, "Then I suppose your great grandfather lived here before your grandfather." When the King nodded in the affirmative, the monk explained, "Whoever was residing here, lived his life believing himself to be the owner of this place; when in fact he had been merely a guest. The palace in which you are living today is going to be occupied by someone else after some years. When that's the case, if this is not a guest house, then what is it?"

This story indicates that we all are merely guests on this Earth. When you too live this life considering yourself to be a guest, the words of the monk will prove very beneficial and you will be liberated from attachment with all worldly things. Even if you have bought objects including a house with your own money, yet it belongs to this world, and you have to leave all of it while departing from this world. Always remind yourself that you are a guest on this Earth and have come here for a short visit.

Therefore, make use of everything available to you, but do not let any of these things use you. Use your mind too, but do not let the mind use you. Don't let it become your master; remember you are its master. If there is no attachment, the mind can be your best friend, but with attachment it will enslave you and become your worst enemy. Hence, live like a guest in this world and be thankful for the hospitality provided to you.

4

Attachment to Wealth

Some people are masters of their wealth, and for some, wealth is their master. When your wealth becomes your master, then it becomes as dangerous as an unrestrained mind. When the mind is restless and unsteady, attachment to wealth increases. And attachment to wealth is a major obstacle in our life. We need to break this attachment through contemplation. With in-depth reflection, we should also get rid of wrong habits like carelessness towards wealth, laziness, not saving enough, squandering, or excessive attachment to wealth.

Attachment or obsession for wealth gives birth to a miser, who only thinks about money day and night. Excessive attachment or desire for wealth makes one a mere security guard of wealth. That is why Laxmi should be accompanied by Narayana. This means along with wealth, you should have understanding of the Supreme Truth, so that obsession with wealth can be eradicated. When you live only in the world of wealth and imagination, you will turn a blind eye to the light of Truth. The following story will help us understand this very important point.

There was a bank clerk who had a nice family consisting of his wife and two children. But most of the time he was unhappy due to shortage of money. He always used to dream of becoming a rich man and was often lost in fantasies of wealth. He used to think that a miracle should occur and somehow he should find a treasure, so that his money problems could end once and for all. One night he was feeling particularly unhappy and cried out with all his heart: "O God! Why didn't you make everyone rich? When will I find a treasure trove?"

The next morning when he woke up and opened his front door, he was shocked to find a huge bag filled with money lying at his doorstep. He was ecstatic thinking God had finally answered his prayers! Overflowing with excitement, he called his wife and narrated the whole story to her. To celebrate their good fortune, he told her to order food from the finest restaurant in town. He then decided that he no longer needed his job. He typed his resignation letter and told his teenage son to go to the bank and hand it over to the bank manager.

Meanwhile his wife informed him that the restaurant was closed. After some enquiry, they found out that all the restaurants in the town were closed. His son returned from the bank and reported that the bank manager had also put in his resignation letter and the assistant manager too was on leave. Then his wife informed him that their daughter was feeling sick. But all the medical stores, clinics, and hospitals too were found to be closed.

> With all this chaos, it came to light that every person in the town had found a bagful of money at their doorsteps. Hence the whole town including all shops, banks, firms, and other places of work were closed. Nobody had gone for work.
>
> Thus, his prayer had been answered, but the solution of his choice for eradicating problems had given birth to another set of problems. Feeling extremely disturbed and agitated, he suddenly woke up. He was relieved beyond words on realizing that it was only a dream. However, this dream had given him a profound insight and his heart filled with gratitude. Folding his hands in reverence, he said, "Dear God, please forgive me. Whatever is happening in this world is perfect. Don't listen to my ideas and imaginations, do what you feel is right for all of us."

This story conveys many important points. There is no denying that money is important in our life, but we should give it importance only to the extent that is necessary. Otherwise we start regarding money as everything and develop an unhealthy attachment towards it. The existence of money is only for ease and convenience of transactions, but today we have forgotten this fundamental fact. That is why we get attached to money and consider it as our ultimate goal. It's time to wake up and understand the purpose of money. Also we need to be ready to earn money in the right way, without trying to avoid hard work. Additionally it's essential to develop awareness about wealth and learn the secrets of abundance*. This

---

* We can learn all about abundance from the book *The Source... Power of Happy Thoughts.*

will help us to achieve prosperity and get rid of money-related worries as well as excessive attachment to wealth.

From the above story we also understood that many a time we entertain wrong ideas and desires due to attachment. We may search for shortcuts too, i.e. illegitimate and easy ways to solve our problems. On realizing that our prayers had emerged from a very limited intellect, we understand our mistake. Hence, whenever we pray, we should certainly contemplate whether the fulfillment of this prayer will prove to be harmful to anyone or to nature.

For example, a person always thinks, "Alas! If only money grew on trees. I would have done so many things. I would have built a huge mansion for my family, bought the most expensive car in the world, gifted my wife with the finest jewels and clothes, and lived a life of unlimited luxury." However, he fails to realize that if money grew on trees, from where would he have found the laborers to construct his mansion? Who would have been ready to work? Who would have come to clean his huge house?

Thus, it is essential to break attachment—first from thoughts, second from objects, third from dependency on people, and fourth from the body. Attachment to objects (which includes houses and wealth) has already been discussed. The remaining three attachments are discussed in detail in the ensuing chapters. For now, two points need to be kept in mind: Firstly, attachment with these four should break. Secondly, freedom from attachment does not mean that you should not attain any of these things. You should achieve whatever you desire—be it health, wealth, love, skills, creativity, etc.—but they should all come packaged in the 'box of detachment'. This means there should be no attachment, obsession, craving, or ego associated with them. Therefore, offer the right prayer to the Almighty, which can be in the following words:

"Dear God! Let everything come to me in the box of detachment.

Please help me attain what you have made for me.

And bless me so that these may facilitate in the expression of my highest self.

Thank You... Thank You... Thank You."

In this prayer, the gift packing or the box of detachment means that whatever you may attain in life, you should not get attached to it, because attachment eventually leads to suffering. With wrong prayers, we may attain everything, but happiness will evade us. Hence detachment from attachment is essential.

5

Attachment to People

We have a tendency to develop attachment and dependency on people and our support system. We don't even realize when the love for our near and dear ones turns into attachment. That is why we may remain sad throughout our life if a loved one passes away. If we had true love for that person and not just attachment, and if we had knowledge of life after death*, we would not have been in sorrow. Thus, attachment and ignorance of the truth can be found hidden at the root of every sorrow.

When we are dependent on the people around us and if we need the support of someone else for every work, we start becoming lazy and begin to avoid work. People start exploiting this weakness. They make us do things according to their whims and we gradually become their slaves. Therefore, don't be attached and dependent on people. This does not mean that you should not take help from others. It only means that you should make efforts to become self-reliant and independent. When needed, you may lend support and also seek support. But if you want to live free, if you want to

---

* You can gain clarity about life after death in the books *Beyond Life* and *Master of Siddhartha*.

remain happy by making others happy, if you want to defeat sorrow and always be blissful, then achieve liberation from attachment as soon as possible.

One usually feels sympathetic towards the visually challenged or blind people, but one's sympathy does not arise for those who are blinded by attachment. However, when you come to know the ill-effects of attachment, you will feel like doing something for those who are blinded by attachment, illusion, and ignorance. You would earnestly beseech them to not be blinded by attachment, but be bonded to God. Let us understand this with the help of a story.

> There was a woman who, blinded by attachment, had never allowed her daughter to step out of the house. Due to her fear and fixation, she had made her daughter weak and vulnerable. One day, in order to escape the suffocating atmosphere of her house, the girl ran away to a relative. But this relative was a bad man. He sold her off to some person. The girl then tried to run away from there too, but was unsuccessful. This other person also tried to sell her off. Traders of flesh started putting a price on her.
>
> At that point of time, a devotee of God happened to be passing by. Seeing the situation, he bid on this girl and succeeded in buying her. He then wrote a message for her on a piece of paper which he asked his companion to deliver, and then walked away. The girl read the message with trepidation. It stated: "Now you are free. You can go wherever you want." Tears started flowing from her eyes and she asked the address of the kind-hearted man from the

messenger. The messenger asked why she wanted to know his address. The girl replied she would like to spend the rest of her life in the service of that man of God.

So, the girl, who wanted to run away from every place, had become ready to spend her whole life in service. This was not because of attachment, illusion, or ignorance, but because of love. This story shows that you can win over people, but for that you don't need attachment, illusion, ignorance, wealth, or force. Instead you need unconditional love and compassion. Devotees of God see only God in others and are therefore able to give unconditional love easily. They are free from attachment and work on freeing others from attachment who are blinded by it.

Let's ask ourselves: Would we want to remain attached by keeping people attached to us, or would we like to be free by making them free?

Thus, it is important to attain freedom from our attachment to people as well as people's attachment to us.

6

Attachment to Problems and Events

If there is some problem or some incident that has occurred in your life, due to which you are feeling distressed, then let us learn some methods that will help you in those situations.

The first method is to use a new television. New television? Yes. The usual television brings close to you all those things that are far off. But this new television that we are talking about will push those things far off that are now close to you and troubling you. Let us consider an example to understand this technique.

Suppose somebody hurled abuses at you, or you have lost something, or you have failed, or something was stolen from you. You are very disturbed. In that situation, just think and imagine what will be your reaction to this incident a year from now. And then try to look at it the same way right now. Do you think you will be as unhappy about it as you are today, even after a year? If this incident looks too insignificant to disturb you after a year, then why not look at it the same way at present? By asking these questions and using the new television to see your reaction in the future, you will be able to easily accept most of your problems and avoid getting attached to them.

So, whenever a negative incident occurs, just ask yourself: "How will I be looking at this incident after one year? How much will this event be affecting me a year from now? Can I look at it the same way right now as I would a year later?"

When you use this new television technique with success, later you will often find yourself saying, "It's good those incidents occurred in my life. Because of those events, something new got created by me and some new possibilities opened up." To attain this conviction, take a look at the events that occurred in your life a year ago. One year is a good time to break attachment to an incident. For example, a year ago a man was miserable on losing his job. Today he is happy with his new business. Now he is thinking that it's good that he was fired from his job. If that had not happened, he may not have been doing business today or achieving success in it.

There may be numerous such examples that may have occurred with you or others, which will reveal the truth: *No event occurs in your life to make you happy or unhappy. It comes to awaken you and push you ahead.* That is why, do not get attached to any event and feel bad about it. Instead awaken your understanding. With the right understanding, you can detach from events and use them for your growth and progress.

Mantra for Every Event

If you have sorrow in your life, what or who is the cause? Is it your neighbor, money, the stars, destiny, the karma of your previous births, your relatives, or is it yourself? Contemplate this question.

Once you know the real cause of sorrow, bliss will always be with you, just as your name is always with you. To know the real cause of sorrow, let us consider the following analogy.

> Suppose you are studying in school in the fifth grade and there is a very mischievous boy in your class. You are very good in studies, while that boy is quite the opposite. That is why he keeps troubling you all the time. However, he does not leave any evidence of his mischief, due to which you are unable to catch him or complain to anyone. But you are sure that whatever untoward is happening with you, this boy is responsible for it. You get very angry but then calm down thinking that you have to tolerate him for only a year as anyway he will fail in his exams and won't be in your class in the next grade. You are shocked to find him with you the next year too. How did this happen?!
>
> Similarly, you want sorrow to fail, but how does it pass? If we consider the mischievous boy to be sorrow, then you don't want the company of sorrow, but you find it accompanying you almost all the time. How did this happen?
>
> On trying to find the reason, the secret was revealed. When the exam was going on, the naughty boy was sitting just behind you. Unconsciously, without realizing it, you had allowed him to copy from your answer paper. Bliss was sitting right next to you, but you hid your paper from him. The result was that bliss failed and sorrow passed. If you continue to repeat this mistake in every test and never find the reason of your sorrow, then sorrow will always follow

you like a shadow.

In the above analogy, as already stated the mischievous boy is sorrow, which always tags behind you and troubles you all the time. You pray for freedom from it, but in unconsciousness your behavior is exactly the opposite. You yourself invite sorrow, although you keep praying that it should not appear in your life.

You must break this unconsciousness right away. Do not show your answer paper to the one sitting behind you. In other words, become alert towards sorrow. Without your permission, sorrow cannot follow you in your life. *Unless you allow it, no one can make you miserable.* You may not be able to stop the occurrence of an incident. However, you can definitely choose what you want to feel about the incident—happy or sad. Nobody can prevent you from making that choice. The choice is yours whether you want to feel joy or sorrow.

You may not be able to prevent the theft of your shoes from outside the temple, but no thief can stop you from choosing to not wear somebody else's shoes instead. No thief can stop you from thinking positive despite the theft. This means no one can prevent you from being happy in any situation. If you want to, you can always be happy. Therefore, choose to be happy, no matter what.

In every incident of your life, recite the following mantra:

"Let bliss succeed and let sorrow fail."

This mantra is the second method of detaching from painful events. Whenever sorrow tries to overpower you, tell yourself: "Sorrow is succeeding; I will not allow it to succeed in any condition!" When you are attached and dependent on someone or something, you are actually chanting the opposite mantra: "Let sorrow pass and let bliss fail." It's crucial to make the right use of mantras. The next time you feel anger or stress, or if you feel sorrow due to attachment, recite the right mantra: "Let bliss succeed and let sorrow fail." Recite this mantra and make every effort to ensure that misery does not succeed in your life. Change your feeling at once and remind yourself, "While I cannot change this incident that has occurred, I can certainly choose how I want to feel about it."

Questions to Convert Sorrow into Bliss

Now let us take a look at the third method of dealing with events.

Every day, every moment, there are numerous incidents happening around you. During or after those incidents, do you feel good or bad? Does bliss succeed or fail? All of us would like to feel good within. Then the question arises: How can you feel good every day and in every event? So let's work on this, due to which your perception of life will change and your world will become beautiful.

After an incident has occurred, you either feel good or bad. In either case, ask yourself: "Where do I experience this good or bad feeling? Is it within my body or somebody else's body?" If that feeling is occurring in somebody else's body, you cannot do anything about it. However, if the bad feeling is occurring within your body, ask yourself the next question: "Who is responsible for feeling in this manner? And if this feeling has to be changed, who can change it? The President of our country? Or me and only me?"

When you ask yourself these questions, you will get the following insights:

1. Every feeling is experienced within our body.
2. We alone are responsible for what we are feeling inside and not anybody else in the world.
3. If the bad feelings have to be changed, we have to change them; nobody else can do it.

If you have grasped these insights, ask yourself, "Henceforth, how will I feel during unpleasant or sorrowful events? Will I feel what I want to or something else?"

If your answer is: "I'll feel bad," then question yourself, "Am I ready to change this feeling?"

If you are ready, ask yourself, "When and where am I going to change it?" The answer will be: "Here and now." Because bliss is always with you—here and now.

It does not take time to change your feeling. If you want, you can instantly change your negative feelings. This will totally change your outlook towards the world. If you are under the impression that somebody else is responsible for your suffering, then you will never be happy.

Hereafter, every moment and in every incident, be aware and ask yourself the questions mentioned above. After answering those questions, you will find that you have started feeling happy, and you are responsible for that feeling too. Thus, a few questions, a mantra, and a new 'television' can always keep you happy.

Detachment from Attachment

Bliss will succeed and sorrow will fail.
Bliss is a sacred place; sorrow is a jail.
Bliss arises from pure wisdom.
Sorrow results from wrong beliefs and misconceptions.

7

Attachment to Thoughts

We develop attachment to our thoughts too. We are captivated by every thought that appears in our mind, get attached to them, and indulge in them repeatedly. Due to this tendency, if we were indulging in unhappy thoughts, then those very thoughts keep recurring time and again. If these thoughts happen to be of depression, then attachment and identification with such thoughts can even lead to death. Thus, this is a very serious matter.

That is why we should not fall prey to our thoughts, instead we should become their pilot. Unfortunately, everyone in this world has fallen prey to thoughts. If you practice meditation* and witness your thoughts as separate from you, then the glue that attaches you to thoughts begins to dissolve. Two meditation techniques are given below which will help you to witness thoughts with detachment. Practice of these meditations will prove to be highly beneficial in disidentifying from thoughts. Try it for yourself and see the results.

---

* You can read more about meditation in the books *Complete Meditation, You Are Meditation,* and *100% Meditation.*

Thought Meditation

1. Close your eyes and sit in the meditation posture. Your spine should be erect but without any strain. You can place your fingers in the *Gyan Mudra* or Wisdom Posture. In this mudra, the hands are placed on the knees with the palms facing upwards. The tips of the index finger and thumb touch each other and the rest of the fingers are kept straight.

2. With eyes closed, start watching your thoughts. See which thoughts are going on in your mind.

3. Keeping the body steady, continue watching the types of thoughts that are passing, from a distance—without getting identified with them and remaining separate. Do not go after any thought. Just watch them passing by. In this process, you will come to know what kind of thoughts go on in your mind, and what thoughts are passing about various topics.

4. Continue to watch and know your thoughts like a witness. Don't label any thought as good or bad. Avoid any such desire that "I want more thoughts" or "I don't want any thoughts."

5. Initially practice this meditation for 5 minutes and gradually go on increasing its duration. When you become an expert in this meditation, then start giving numbers to your thoughts.

Thought Numbering Meditation

1. In order to attain a thoughtless state, in this meditation thoughts are eliminated by giving sequential numbers. Sit

in the meditation posture and close your eyes. Begin the meditation by watching every thought.

2. Now start numbering every thought. As soon as one thought arises, number it in your mind as 'one.' As the second thought arises, number it as 'two.' In this way, count all your thoughts.

3. Continue to watch quietly even when there are no thoughts. If you feel, "At this time I don't have any thoughts," then number it too because it is also a thought.

4. Don't pursue any thought. Just number it and leave it.

5. With this meditation, there will be a radical reduction in the number of thoughts. Sometimes even a thoughtless state will manifest. However, practice this meditation regularly without expecting a given result.

These two meditations are very effective in detaching from thoughts.

Other Methods to Detach from Thoughts

Another technique to detach from thoughts is to look at your thoughts as if they are your children. When children start troubling you, you teach them to be quiet. In the same way, when thoughts come and trouble you repeatedly, you can train them to be quiet. Just like attachment to their children often becomes the cause of sorrow for their parents, likewise, attachment to your thoughts can become the cause of your misery.

If kids clutch your hand and insist on going out at odd times, you usually pacify them by saying, "Go and play now, we'll go out later."

The same way if thoughts appear at any time and insist to drag you into the feelings of misery, greed, hatred, or fear, you can tell them, "Go and play now, we'll entertain those feelings later on."

Don't allow any thought to appear and snatch away your happiness. Don't let sorrow and misery enter your life. This can be accomplished only when you learn to watch your thoughts in the right manner. Suppose you notice a few gray strands in your hair and a thought pops up at once: "I am growing old... I'm looking so old…" Tell that thought, "Ok, dear. Now go out and play." Do not pick this thought up in your lap, i.e. do not entertain it and don't believe it to be true; otherwise it will actually make you old.

The day the thought of "growing old" or "looking old" engulfs you, you start feeling weak from that day onwards. This is what happens when you are unable to detach from thoughts. Also, you mistakenly believe all the thoughts that appear in your mind to be true. Instead, why not think, "What happened in just one day?" Until yesterday you were young and strong, and then you saw a gray hair and a thought popped up, and you started feeling weak right away. This is the power of thoughts. Therefore, as soon as you get a thought like "I am growing old," just say to it, "Ok kid, go out and play," and detach from it. If you get attached to that thought, it will affect your body.

Therefore, understand the power of thoughts, turn them into positive ones, and utilize them to your advantage. If you are attached to negative thoughts and are constantly entertaining them, then the power of thoughts begins to work against you, and may even lead to premature death.

If kids constantly insist on being picked up and held in your arms, you don't oblige them every time. Similarly, do not pay attention to thoughts or entertain them all the time. Thoughts of anger or hatred are like devilish kids, but they are kids. Don't pick them up in your lap. Avoid getting attached to them as well as pampering or entertaining them. Don't let them trouble you. Instead try to teach them a lesson by saying "What did you say? Ok, great. We'll discuss this later. Now go out and play." Or you may say, "I will listen to you too, but now sit in silence for 10 minutes." By sitting in silence, you will start becoming aware and alert towards your thoughts. You will begin to realize how many kids (thoughts) you have. Meditation and watching thoughts with awareness will soon detach you from thoughts and also protect you from the impact of negative thoughts.

You may have seen that mischievous children who are spoilt are difficult to control and may even become criminals on growing up. Likewise, if restless thoughts are constantly entertained and pampered, they can make you commit any kind of sin. Just as you read 'child training' books to train your kids, in the same way you need to study 'thought training' books** or enroll in a school (*satsang*) where thoughts can be trained.

When we get attached to thoughts, we also get attached to our imaginations and perceptions. People get attached to their imagination and perception of God and become opposed to other religions. Racism and violence related to caste or religion are basically due to such attachment.

** You can read about thoughts and laws of thought in the book *The Source... Power of Happy Thoughts*.

Additionally, we get attached to our ideas and suggestions too. Due to this attachment, we try to prove that only our ideas and suggestions are correct. If others do not accept our suggestions, we get angry. If someone steals our idea and touts it as their own, we may get violent. Hence, we should be careful while uttering words such as 'my thought,' 'my opinion,' 'my idea,' or 'my suggestion.' Detachment helps in avoiding the above-mentioned issues.

8

Balancing Head and Heart for Detachment

Attachment is eradicated if the heart and discriminative intelligence (*viveka*) are used in an apt and balanced manner. Discriminative intelligence is a symbol of understanding, intelligence, and thinking power. Heart is a symbol of love, experience, and feeling. When living in this world, if you use only your head, you will get more and more entangled in the web of illusion and attachment. By connecting the head with the heart, you can break out of this web. Let's read a little story to understand this further.

> A young man was very tense due to some family issues. To get some air, he decided to take a walk on the beach, which was some distance from his home. At the beach, he saw an old person sitting quietly on a boulder and fishing. He walked past that old person to the far segment of the beach. He then started pacing to and fro trying to think of how to handle his problems. By the time he decided to go home, the sun was about to set.
>
> As he was returning, he found the old person still sitting at

his spot. Therefore, he asked, "Did you catch anything?" The old man nodded his head and said, "Yes." The young man inquired further, "What did you catch?" The old man put one hand on his head and the other on his heart. Not understanding the meaning of this gesture, the young man asked what was he trying to convey?

The old man replied, "I was sitting here looking at the sea, sky, waves, fish, sun, and the whole world. Looking at all of this, I thought that if God is operating this world and looking after all these things, then he must be doing the same for me as well. So, if he is operating me and looking after me, then what do I have to do?!

"Further I thought that he must be giving thoughts and feelings from within to make us function. These feelings are felt through the heart, and it is due to these feelings that all activities are being carried out in the world. I too am able to function due to these feelings. Even for simple activities like walking or sitting, God is giving me thoughts.

"This is what I was able to catch today. That's why I kept one hand on the head and the other on the heart. So what if I did not catch any fish, I caught hold of my head and heart. God has given us intellect so that we can think about all this and he has given us the heart so that we can experience these secrets."

The young man was touched by these insights. On hearing these words, all his troubles vanished and he returned home liberated from attachment.

You too can be liberated from attachment by making the right use of the head and the heart. While walking, sitting, or doing anything, observe how God is making you function! What kind of experience is he making you feel within your heart!

If you can realize this secret as to why you are given thoughts and feelings, then you will always remain happy. Fishing was merely an excuse for the old man. Your life too is only an excuse or a medium to learn the supreme truth. Realizing the truth is the basic purpose of human life. Use your discriminative intelligence and your heart in a balanced and ideal manner to attain permanent detachment from attachment. That's when you will start abiding in your true, divine nature.

9

Attachment to Fruit of Actions

When we do something, we expect a given result. Most of our actions, deeds, or karma—be it at work or home or anywhere else—are done with some expectations or desires. Sometimes we are aware of our expectations and desires and sometimes we are not because they are too subtle. In either case, we have attachment to our karma and its fruit.

The *Bhagavad Gita* says: "Perform your karma without concerning yourself with the fruit of your karma." Taoism says: "Act without expectation." But what is wrong with desiring the fruit of our actions and why should we act without expectation?

The reason is that expectation is one of the major causes of stress, disappointment, frustration, anger, irritation, depression, and discouragement. When things don't happen as we expect them to and when people don't behave as we expect them to, such feelings arise.

When we are distanced from our true divine self, we build expectations for the results of our actions. We seek instant gratification of desires, we expect people to respond positively, we wish for approval, praise, gratitude, respect, recognition, and so on. When this does not happen, we sink into negative feelings.

The reality is that each one of our actions yields corresponding fruit. And no one can escape action. Even if you do nothing all day and all night, you cannot escape its fruit because 'doing nothing' is also an action. Some results appear instantly while others are delayed. Since many actions yield delayed results, people become frustrated or disappointed and stop performing those actions.

When we perform an action for the first time, our focus is on the action, because we are not yet aware of its result. We perform the action with intuitive thought, resulting in our best performance. But as soon as we see the result of our action, our focus shifts to the result. We create an impression of the result in our mind. The next time we perform the same action, we hold onto our past impression of the result. Due to this, we do not act intuitively to the best of our ability. The result is invariably different from the previous one, causing negative feelings. Therefore, it's better to avoid carrying any expectations of the fruit of action because non-fulfillment can cause sorrow.

But that's not all. The irony is that expecting a particular result causes suffering not only when it remains unfulfilled, but also when it *is* fulfilled. When the fruit is received as expected, it boosts the ego. The ego is reinforced with the belief that it can control the result. The next time the ego tries to fix the outcome of action and attempts to control the result. This causes stress while you perform action and strengthens the focus on the fruit, rather than the action. Additionally, subsequent episodes of non-fulfillment become more painful.

How to Perform Actions

So, how should we perform our actions? A story from old folklore will help us to understand this crucial aspect of our life.

> Once it so happened that the Gods were angry with mankind and decided that there shall be no rainfall on Earth. This had a drastic effect on not just the humans but all flora and fauna on the planet. Agriculture was particularly affected by this drought and all the farmers were depressed, except for one. This one farmer continued to plough the fields as before. Some people were baffled and others amazed by this feat. The farmer continued to do this for three years of the drought, until one day the villagers approached him and asked the reason for doing so. They thought he was doing it out of blind hope. But the answer of the farmer surprised them.
>
> He said, "This effort is not out of blind hope or some expectation of fruit. I am ploughing the fields regularly because I fear that I may forget the art of ploughing if I don't continue to do it in wait for the rains." These words reached the heavens and made it to the ears of Lord Indra—the God of rain. Hearing these words, Lord Indra wondered, "If what the farmer says is true, i.e. we tend to forget something when we are out of touch with it, does that apply to me too? After all, I haven't made the rain fall on Earth since the last three years." Realizing his folly, Indra immediately decided to exercise his power, and lo and behold, there

was rain on Earth! The earnest effort of the farmer was rewarded.

What is this power that the farmer had within him? In the battle of Kurukshetra, this is the same power that Lord Krishna introduced to Arjuna when He said, "Perform your karma without concerning yourself with the fruit of your karma." This power is called as *Indifferent Enthusiasm*.

Normally, the indifference that one experiences from depression is negative and lacks in any positive energy. But there is another kind of indifference that comes from the joy one has in knowing one's true divine self and operating from the Self.

Indifference and enthusiasm seem contradictory but are actually not. In fact, the enthusiasm that comes from indifference has long term sustenance. Just like profound change comes from stillness and peace, and not from war. This indifference comes when our focus is only on doing our karma. The essence is there should be enthusiasm towards action but indifference when it comes to expecting its results.

This implies that the mind needs to be trained to focus on completing the action with total involvement and without focusing on the outcomes. When action is done with total involvement, usually the right outcomes will naturally follow. What's crucial is keeping principle focus on doing action and not on its result. This is akin to telling a child that if he studies well, he will get the reward of watching the circus in town. Now, instead of studying, if the child thinks all day long about the circus, will he study well?

Once, a man went to Nisargadatta Maharaj and asked him, "Why do you still need to sing devotional songs when you have already attained Self realization?" Nisargadatta smiled and said, "I do it because my Guru had asked me to. He then passed away and I was never told to stop. Therefore, I do it without any expectation of benefit from it but with full enthusiasm." There is an indifference in this and yet an enthusiasm.

Let's take another example.

When Ramana Maharshi after realizing his true self went to stay in the mountains, people followed him there and soon he realized the need of an ashram. He was very enthusiastic with regards to the creation of the ashram and wanted to ensure it was well-built, and hence he personally supervised it. However, he was totally indifferent to whether it was popular and whether people were visiting it because he knew the secret. By being indifferent to the result, you are not left empty handed. In fact, you get the result you want because all attention is focused on doing the right actions which lead to it.

Let not the thoughts of the future and its uncertainties distract you. Let not over-pessimism shake you. What's important is that we continue our deeds even under adverse circumstances, for only then lies the possibility of results. We must remember the farmer who sows seeds every year even when he's not sure whether they will sprout due to the uncertainty of rainfall. He knows for sure that without sowing them, there is no possibility for them to sprout. Mother Nature operates on this principle and there are no exceptions to this.

Self-realized souls know well the secret of enthusiastic action. They are often intensely involved in what needs to be done and people around them tend to think that this enthusiasm is because they are interested in achieving something. However, for them, all action is like a divine play and they are often detached to the results that their actions yield. This makes them free from tension, due to which they are able to draw inspiration and operate from the source of true creativity.

A true understanding of this principle will teach us to pray for receiving the fruit in the box of detachment.

In the state of indifferent enthusiasm, the mind will always be in the state of uncertainty about the result of action and thus will realize that it is futile to worry about it and would let it happen. From this seeming uncertainty and the space of the unknown, something new and creative emerges. By and by, we will learn the art of being comfortable in the space of 'not knowing.' Answers to questions on marriage, children, success in career, etc. will be answered at their own good time if we do not run behind them. You will not run behind them but they will come to you because you continue doing your karma enthusiastically.

If you learn to live calmly amidst uncertainty, it will make you a magnet of peace. This magnet will attract gifts from the unknown that excessive striving and thinking will not lead to. The great unknown is the source of creativity and possibility.

The Ultimate Fruit

One may wonder that if expectations about the result need to be avoided, then does that mean we can't hope for anything at all while being engaged in action? Forgoing expectations without understanding the truth completely and in depth can lead to negative outcomes such as dullness and lack of purpose. It can also lead to misunderstandings. You may say, "How can I feel motivated to do something if I can't expect anything good in return?" or "Should I work hard at my job but not expect a salary in return?"

Focusing on the result is inherently flawed and occurs due to ignorance of your true nature. The reality is that your essence is divine and blissful. You postpone your joy to the future attainment of the fruit. *True joy is never a result of action. Joy is your true nature. You cannot do something to gain joy. Rather the innate joy that is experienced in the awareness of who-you-truly-are naturally touches whatever you do.*

Joy is an essential attribute of the Self. When you are in Self-awareness, you experience unconditional joy. You don't need to do something to gain happiness. Being alive itself becomes a cause for celebration. Actions inspired from the Self then happen through your body, which lead to the best creations and best outcomes.

This can be a paradigm shift. We always act to attain joy. It will feel very relaxing to know that you can act from joy, instead of acting for joy. Instead of running towards the finish line (of happiness), you can begin from the finish line.

Also remember that in your daily dealings and interactions, you are giving to the Self and receiving from the Self. *You are dealing only with the Self. People are merely channels through which your interaction with the Self takes place.* So, if at all you desire the fruit of your actions, expect it from the Self, not from anyone else. And as long as you are expecting from the omnipotent Self, why not desire for the ultimate fruit? What is the ultimate or the highest fruit? It's enlightenment or Self realization. The aspiration for enlightenment will liberate you from all other desires. It will lead you to get established in your divine blissful nature.

10

Attachment to the Body

We may like our body or not, but in either case we have deep attachment to our body. We lead our life based on the premise that we are the body and so are the others. Therefore, it's time to know the truth about the body.

The human body is made up of four sheaths or walls. Within the four walls, in the center is your true self, the Self, or the real 'I'—which is formless and limitless. Thus, the supreme truth is that you are not the body, you are **in** the body. When, due to ignorance of the truth, you believe 'I' means 'my body', that's when you develop the biggest attachment of all—attachment to the body. Assuming yourself to be the body is the biggest ignorance.

Always remember you are using your body; you are not the body. Whenever there is any pain in the body, or you feel attachment towards the body, recite the mantra: *"I am in the body; I am not the body."* This mantra will increase your tolerance and endurance. Additionally, this mantra will reduce your attachment and identification with the body, as well as raise your level of happiness. If you forget this mantra, attachment will once again raise its head. Then you have to become aware again and recite the mantra once more. In fact, keep on repeating it whenever you remember. With constant efforts in this manner, you can achieve detachment from the body too.

Self and the Body

In case you are wondering why detachment from the body is important, let's consider an analogy.

> Suppose your body is a pen. The Self or the real you created this pen to write its own story. But the interesting thing about this pen is that it has the ability to write its own story too. If the Self doesn't hold the pen correctly and clutches it too tightly, then the harmony between the Self and the pen is lost, and the pen starts writing its own story. This leads to suffering and also the purpose of creating the pen is not fulfilled. However, if the Self holds the pen lightly in an optimum manner, then it can use the pen for writing the story it wants to, which leads to everlasting joy and bliss.

Now let's understand what this analogy means. The Self or the 'real you' is without form or shape. Hence, the Self created the body so that it could experience and express itself. However, if the Self or the real you get tightly and deeply attached to the body, then you become identified with the body. You forget your formless divine nature as well as the purpose of the body. You begin to consider yourself to be the body. The body has its own desires and beliefs, and since you are identified with it, you feel as if those desires and beliefs are yours. Therefore, you start operating and leading your life according to those beliefs and desires. In other words, the pen starts writing its own story. The body desires sensual pleasures, comforts, and luxuries. It develops attachment to objects, people, events, thoughts, image, and to itself (body). Thus begins the game of joy and sorrow. An entire lifetime can be lost in vain due to your attachment and identification with the body.

To break this attachment, the Self needs to hold the pen in the right manner. Its hold should be light. This means you should not attach tightly to the body, instead your connection to it should be light with just a little distance in between. You need to develop detachment from the body. In order to do so, you should observe whatever is happening in the body or with the body as a detached witness.

For example, if some thoughts or sensations arise within the body, you should observe them from a distance and assert to yourself: "These thoughts and sensations have arisen in the body. I am not the body; I am *in* the body."

If some problem appears or if some feelings arise due to attachment with objects, people, events, or the body, remind yourself: "This is happening with the body, not with me. In fact, all of this is happening not *with* me but *for* me. All these relations or problems have been given to me so that I can train my mind to become pure, loving, unwavering, obedient, and integrated. This will help me return onto myself and experience my true *being*. I can then express my divine qualities, which will lead to divine creations and everlasting bliss. This will fulfill the purpose of creating this body."

Constant practice of witnessing in a detached manner while remembering that you are the formless divine Self will help you in detaching from the body. Meditation will help you in this process. Once you start observing and experiencing yourself to be separate from the body-mind during meditation, you can do the same during everyday activities too. Constant practice or *sadhana* of detached witnessing along with the mantra "I am in the body; I am not the body" will help you to pull away from the cycle of joy and sorrow and get established in your true self. The body will then rightly become your medium to experience and express your true self. This will mark the end of all suffering and the beginning of endless and pure happiness.

Journey from Attachment to Detachment

Let us take a look at how in the journey from being a little child to growing up, attachment develops to objects (non-living) and bodies (living) and how it dissolves.

As a small child: When the child is small, his relationship with everything and everyone is "I and objects – I and objects." In other words, he believes everything to be inanimate or non-living. He picks one object and hits it on another. It makes no difference to him whether a mirror breaks or a heart. Breaking things is normal for him due to childhood and ignorance.

On growing a bit: When the child grows a bit, his relationship with everything is "I and objects – I and you." This means he considers his family members as objects, and inanimate objects as living things. He starts loving his objects like his cell phone, computer, pen, watch, motorcycle, clothes, shoes, etc. And by being stubborn and obstinate, he makes use of people like objects. He does not care at all about their feelings.

On becoming a bit mature: When the child becomes a bit mature and sensible, his relationship with everything becomes: "I and you – I and object." This means he starts giving more importance to relations and people as compared to objects. He begins to understand the feelings of people. Love for others begins to awaken within him.

On becoming a bit more mature: When he grows up and attains some more maturity, then his relationship with everything becomes: "I and you – I and you." This means in addition to giving respect to people, he also starts respecting inanimate objects. This is because now he is aware and he believes that the same vibration which is present in living beings is also present in objects. Hence, he stops throwing things around and begins to handle them with care. Pure and unconditional love begins to awaken in his heart.

On becoming quite mature: On attaining spiritual wisdom, he becomes quite mature, and then his relationship with everything starts becoming as: "Object and object – object and object." This means he realizes that until now he used to think of his body as 'I' and the body of the other person as 'you'. In reality, 'I' and 'you' are not bodies, but we had been interacting with each other like I am a body and you are also a body. In other words, an object was interacting with another object. After reaching this stage, he begins to understand the last stage.

On becoming fully mature: After attaining supreme wisdom, which is beyond knowledge and ignorance, he becomes fully mature. Subsequently, his relationship with everything is "You and You – You and You." This means he sees God or the Supreme Consciousness in everyone and everything. In this state, 'I' ceases to exist, that is why there is no question of attachment to anyone or anything. Thus, attachment is totally annihilated.

Contemplating in this manner and beginning the journey to attain the supreme truth will lead to complete detachment from attachment. This will subsequently lead to liberation and unbroken bliss.

11

Who Can Help in Detachment

A true Guru is the only one who can help you detach from attachment. Thus, attaining a Guru or spiritual master is the most important event of life. You cannot even imagine at this time how a true Guru can become the gateway to take you from attachment to complete liberation.

If you are seeking a guru who can help you attain some relief from your worldly problems, then you will not get liberated from attachment; on the contrary you will get even more glued to attachment. People go to such gurus for getting relief from their problems and not for purifying and cleansing their minds. Those gurus give them some ritual, talisman or rosary, some words, some auspicious time, some ashes, or some *prasad* (an offering made to God which is then distributed among devotees). People are pleased to receive such things and find some respite from their troubles.

On the other hand, if you are in search of a true Guru, only then you will attain liberation from attachment, which will lead to permanent freedom from all suffering. If this has touched your heart, then contemplate on it at once and take action. Pray to God (in whatever form you believe) for attaining a true Guru or master.

If there is thirst in your prayer, the Guru himself/herself will find you. Only God can detach you from attachment. And in order to do so, God communicates with you through the Guru. Once you get your Guru, then let him work in your life. Just as you have let your parents, siblings, friends, or spouse work in your life, now it's the Guru's turn. Establish a pure and true relationship with your Guru and gain from it. Once you have found your Guru, always abide by his commands.

The Guru helps you to recognize the unlimited power of faith. He fills you with the highest self-confidence. By imparting wisdom, the Guru establishes the conviction within you that: "The one who takes care of his creations living even at the bottom of the sea and sustains them, will definitely take care of you too. Keep faith in that Almighty." Do not become attached and dependent on others; develop attachment with God alone. Attachment with God cuts off the worldly attachment just as poison antidotes poison and diamond cuts diamond. When you have God with you, why do you have to get entangled in attachment and illusion? Why dig a well when you are sitting at the shore of a mighty river? Try to recognize every opportunity that you get in your life. You can achieve everything with divine love and devotion, not with attachment.

12

How to Develop Detachment

As soon as you enter the world, various attachments ensnare you. So, before entering the world of attachment, what should you do? Attachment makes you forget everything—including the wisdom you have attained regarding detachment. Thereafter, all your thoughts, feelings, words, and actions are influenced by attachment.

That is why if you can learn to go into the realm of silence before getting into attachment, you will not take any wrong steps. Suppose due to a feeling of hatred or for protecting something you are attached to, you get a thought of harming someone. Before carrying out such action, if you can go into silence for a while, there is every possibility that you would easily give up that idea. This is because in silence you realize who you actually are and who the other person is. You gain the conviction that the same Self or Consciousness pervades everyone and everything.

Therefore, learn to go into silence before taking any decision. Silence is the best remedy for bringing about a change of heart and detaching from attachment. Any decision that you take in the state of silence will be in the interest of all. In this illusory world, life is like a game of snakes and ladders. Everything you see from a state of attachment is a snake, and everything you see in the state of silence is a ladder. All decisions that you take with attachment will bring you down (cause downfall) and all decisions that you take from inner silence will take you up (lead to true growth and progress).

Releasing Meditation

Another powerful method that can help you let go of attachments is Releasing Meditation. You can record this meditation in your voice and practice it every day. You can also tweak it according to your need of the moment, and on practicing it you will immediately start feeling lighter and happier. So, let's see how to practice this meditation.

Close your eyes and sit in a comfortable meditative posture. Keep your back straight but relaxed. Take a few deep breaths and release them slowly.

Tell yourself, "I am now going to practice meditation. My complete focus will be on this meditation."

With eyes closed, you have to release all that is not needed. Ask yourself, "What is it that I am holding on to and it's now time to let go? What are the attachments that bind me? What are the desires that the mind is holding on to? The time has come to release them." Then ask, "Is it okay to release them? Can I allow myself to let go?" See what answer appears in your heart.

The answer may emerge: "Yes, I can allow myself to let go of everything that binds me and prevents me from experiencing true freedom and everlasting bliss." Whatever you are holding on to, right or wrong, needs to be released. Whatever is for you will come back to you—multiplied. What is not for you will be dissolved. Hence, don't be afraid to let go of your attachments, because there is nothing to lose, but true freedom and happiness to gain.

1. With eyes closed, ask yourself, "Do I harbor deep attachment to my house and objects, which causes misery in one way or the other?" If your answer is yes, and if you are ready to release this attachment, tell yourself, "I am ready to live like a guest on this short visit to Earth. I will happily use all that is available to me without a sense of ownership because all of this is temporary and leads to sorrow. I am letting go of this attachment to house and objects."

   Close your fist and then open it slowly saying, "Let go… let go… let go… Let go, let go, let go… I have released this attachment."

2. Now ask yourself, "Do I consider money to be everything and think about it day and night? Has it become my master and my ultimate goal? Am I dependent on it for my happiness?" If your answer is yes, then ask yourself, "Am I ready to release this obsession with wealth?" If you are, then say to yourself, "I am ready to release this excessive attachment to wealth, as well as wrong habits like carelessness towards money, laziness, not saving enough, squandering, or miserliness. Money is only for ease and convenience of transactions. I am the master of wealth and I believe nature fulfills all my needs in a divine manner. May I attain everything that I

desire in the box of detachment. The Supreme Truth is my ultimate goal, not money. Therefore, I am letting go of all my worries and attachment to wealth."

Close your fist and then open it slowly saying, "Let go… let go… let go… Let go, let go, let go… I have released this attachment."

3. Then ask yourself, "Am I dependent on other people for everything, including my happiness? Have I become a slave to them due to the support and comforts they provide? Has the love for my near and dear ones turned into attachment, weakness, and misery?" If your answer is yes, and if you are ready to get rid of this dependency and attachment, tell yourself, "I am ready to become independent and get rid of this slave-like attitude. I don't want to be blinded by attachment but bonded to God. I want to have unconditional love for everyone, not attachment. I will protect and take care of my children and other near and dear ones in the best possible manner, but I am releasing the attachment because it causes sorrow in my life as well as theirs. I want to live free and make others free. I am letting go of this attachment to people."

Close your fist and then open it slowly saying, "Let go… let go… let go… Let go, let go, let go… I have released this attachment."

4. Ask yourself, "Do I feel distressed by the problems or events that occur in my life? Do I get attached to them and let them affect me deeply leading to sorrow? Am I ready to deal with

them in a different and better manner?" If yes, then say to yourself, "I am ready to look at any event as I would a year from now. I believe that no event occurs in my life to make me happy or unhappy. It comes to awaken me and push me ahead. Hence, I won't get attached to any event or feel bad about it, instead I will use it for my growth and progress. I may not be able to stop the occurrence of an incident, but I can choose how to feel about it. I choose to be happy in every situation. The truth is no one can make me unhappy if I don't want to be. I am responsible for my suffering and I choose to change my negative feelings into positive ones—here and now. My mantra in every event is: '*Let bliss succeed and let sorrow fail.*' I am ready to let go of attachment to every problem or event that troubles me from my past or present."

Close your fist and then open it slowly saying, "Let go… let go… let go… Let go, let go, let go… I have released this attachment."

5. Then ask yourself, "Do I get attached to my thoughts and indulge in them repeatedly—especially the negative ones like guilt, depression, feeling of failure, hatred, etc.? Do I believe all the thoughts that appear in my mind to be true and let them trouble me? Do my restless thoughts make me do wrong things? Do I believe that only *my* perceptions, ideas, and suggestions are correct and *should* be followed, and if they are not, I feel angry?" If your answer is yes to any of these questions and if you are ready to get rid of these issues, then say to yourself, "I am ready to detach from the

thoughts that trouble me and cause negative feelings. I will not entertain them; instead I'll treat them like kids and tell them to go out and play. I will not allow any thought to make me do anything wrong, nor will I force anybody to accept my ideas, suggestions, and perceptions. I am ready to let go of attachment to all my thoughts."

Close your fist and then open it slowly saying, "Let go… let go… let go… Let go, let go, let go… I have released this attachment."

6. Now ask, "Do I consider myself to be the body? And thereby believe that whatever happens with it happens with me? Do I get attached to all the issues related to the body, which make me miserable? Do I also believe others to be the body and treat them as such?" If your answer is yes, and if you are ready to develop detachment towards the body, say, "I am ready to treat the body as what it is—a vehicle for my infinite, divine Self. I am not the body; I am *in* the body. My body is my friend. I will feed it, protect it, and take care of it. But my purpose of coming to Earth is to train my body-mind to become pure, loving, unwavering, obedient, and integrated. That is why I will train my body-mind so that ultimately it can help me to experience and express my true self. That's the purpose of this body. I will always remember who I am and who others are, and I will treat them as such. I am ready to let go of any attachment to the body."

Close your fist and then open it slowly saying, "Let go… let go… let go… Let go, let go, let go… I have released this attachment."

7. Finally tell yourself, "I am letting go of every kind of attachment that I have and whatever I have been holding onto."

   Close your fist and then open it slowly saying, "Let go… let go… let go… I am free... I am free...I am freedom." Slowly open your eyes and start living a detached life.

Practice this meditation every night or any other time suitable for you. Continue practicing it consistently every day and you will soon start seeing its miraculous results. Attachments will gradually begin to loosen and dissolve, and your happiness level will rise.

Forgiveness Prayer

One more very effective and simple method that can help you cut free from attachment is the Forgiveness Prayer. The practice of seeking forgiveness from God or Self can, in fact, help you to attain freedom from any problem or shortcoming. It is a boon indeed. Therefore, offer this prayer as many times as you can but at least once every day.

Dear God,

Please forgive me for assuming myself to be the body-mind

and developing so many attachments.

Forgive me for identifying with the fickle mind

and getting attached to my thoughts, ideas,
and fruit of my work.

Forgive me for attachment to the body, wealth, objects, and people.

Kindly forgive everything and everyone who has contributed to the growth of these attachments, including me.

I pray with all my heart to kindly eliminate all the causes and consequences of attachment.

Please forgive all my karma arising from attachment.

I will put in maximum efforts to avoid repeating this mistake in the future.

Forgive me for forgetting my ultimate purpose of coming to Earth

May my mind become pure, steadfast, loving, and obedient.

May I get established in my original essence.

May I live a truly free life and help others to attain freedom too.

Please bless me with freedom from all attachments

As I am in favour of detachment and total liberation.

I am in favour of true love for all and endless bliss.

I am free… I am free… I am freedom.

Thank You… Thank You… Thank You.

More than the words, it is the feelings imbued in this prayer that cleanse and release the blocks that clog the free flow of life. This prayer will help you to cut the strings of bondage that bind you to people, objects, your thoughts, and your body. As a result, you will begin to live as your true, limitless Self.

Summarizing with 'A Little, But Today'

Give up attachment with understanding. Don't live life full of attachments. It is not difficult to give up and get rid of attachment. In fact, it is quite easy because attachment is not a gem, it is grime. If you attain complete wisdom and are aware of your purpose on Earth, it will be very easy to develop detachment. Just as easily as you breathe out, you can give up all your attachments. No person has any hesitation whatsoever in releasing the breath. One knows that after releasing one breath, the next breath will automatically come in. Likewise, let things come and go smoothly in your life; do not get attached to anything. Pray that whatever you get in life, may you receive it in the box of detachment. Carry out your actions with joy and indifferent enthusiasm—without being anxious about the outcomes. Start using the new 'television'. Repeat the Forgiveness Prayer as much as possible. Before going into the world of attachment, take a dip in silence. Practice the Releasing Meditation regularly. Do not spend your life wearing the crown of attachment. Live a bright detached life and always keep bliss with you. The art of breaking attachments by developing attachment to God has been explained earlier along with several methods, questions, and mantras. With these practices, you will not become a slave to anyone.

The mind may make excuses on seeing so many practices. Therefore, in order to succeed, a little secret that you should tell your mind is: *"A little, but today."* This implies that start using the practices given in this book today itself, even if it's a little bit, and continue this every day. Start observing some of your thoughts right from today. You can start telling your negative thoughts right now to go out and play, just as you may tell your kids. Or you may begin today with the prayers given in this book. Do a little bit, take just a small step, but do it today.

In this way, make small efforts every day to keep bliss within you and sorrow far away. If you start using this secret with perseverance and patience, a day will come when you will attain the ultimate purpose of your life in the school of this world.

If you have understood and liked the wisdom presented in this book, then contemplate on it and implement it. If you don't like some points, or some things don't appear to be very logical to you, don't reject them but keep them parked separately in your mental space for some time. Just like when you are not using your vehicle, you keep it in a parking lot, in the same way keep those points in parking for the time being. A time will come when you will be able to appreciate those points as well and start using them too. So, let's begin this journey of complete detachment from attachment to get established in your true blissful self and attain freedom from suffering.

* * *

You can send your opinion or feedback on this book to:

Tej Gyan Foundation, P.O. Box 25, Pimpri Colony,
Pimpri, Pune – 411017, Maharashtra, INDIA
Email: englishbooks@tejgyan.org

Write for Us

We welcome writers, translators and editors to join our team. If you would like to volunteer, please email us at: englishbooks@tejgyan.org or call: +91 90110 10963

About Sirshree

Sirshree's spiritual quest, which began during his childhood, led him on a journey through various schools of thought and prevalent meditation practices. His overpowering desire to attain the Truth made him relinquish his teaching profession. After a long period of contemplation on the truth of life, his spiritual quest culminated in the attainment of the ultimate truth. Since then, over the last two decades, he has dedicated his life toward elevating mass consciousness and making spiritual pursuit simple and accessible to all.

Sirshree espouses, **"All paths that lead to the truth begin differently, but culminate at the same point – understanding. Understanding is complete in itself. Listening to this understanding is enough to attain the truth."**

Sirshree has delivered more than 3000 discourses that throw light on this understanding, simplify various aspects of life and unravel missing links in spirituality. He delivers the understanding in casual contemporary language by weaving profound aspects into analogies, parables and humor that provoke one to contemplate.

To make it possible for people from all walks of life to directly experience this understanding, Sirshree has designed the *Maha Aasmani Param Gyan Shivir* – a retreat designed as a comprehensive system for imparting wisdom. This system for wisdom, which has been accredited with ISO 9001:2015 certification, has inspired thousands of seekers from all walks of life to progress on their journey of the Truth. This system makes the wisdom accessible to every human being, regardless of religion, caste, social strata, country or belief system.

Sirshree is the founder of Tej Gyan Foundation, a no-profit organization committed to raising mass consciousness with branches in India, the United States, Europe and Asia-Pacific. Sirshree's retreats have transformed the lives of thousands and his teachings have inspired various social initiatives for raising global consciousness.

His published work includes more than 100 books, some of which have been translated in more than 10 languages and published by leading publishers. Sirshree's books provide profound and practical reading on existential subjects like emotional maturity, harmony in relationships, developing self-belief, overcoming stress and anxiety, and dealing with the question of life-beyond-death, to name a few. His literature on core spirituality expounds the deeper meaning of self-realization and self-stabilization, unravelling missing links in the understanding of karma, wisdom, devotion, meditation and consciousness.

Various luminaries and celebrities like His Holiness the Dalai Lama, publishers Mr. Reid Tracy, Ms. Tami Simon and Yoga Master Dr. B. K. S. Iyengar have released Sirshree's books and lauded his work. "The Source" book series, authored by Sirshree, has sold over 10 million copies in 5 years. His book, "The Warrior's Mirror", published by Penguin, was featured in the Limca Book of Records for being released on the same day in 11 languages.

Tejgyan... The Road Ahead
What is Tejgyan?

Tejgyan is the wisdom of the existential truth, which is beyond duality. "Gyan" is a term commonly used for "knowledge". Tejgyan is the wisdom beyond knowledge and ignorance. It is understanding that arises from direct experience of the final truth. It is what sets us free from the limitations of the mind and opens us to our highest potential.

In today's world, there are people who feel disharmony and are desperately trying to achieve balance in an unpredictable life. Tejgyan helps them in harmonizing with their true nature, the Self, thereby restoring balance in all aspects of their lives.

And then, there are those who are successful, but feel a sense of emptiness within. Tejgyan provides them fulfilment and helps them to embark on a journey towards self-realization. There are others who feel lost and are seeking the meaning of life. Tejgyan helps them to realize the true purpose of human life.

All this is possible with Tejgyan due to a very simple reason. The experience of the ultimate truth (God or Pure consciousness) is always available. The direct experience of this truth is possible provided the right method is known. Tejgyan is that method, that understanding.

The understanding of Tejgyan makes it possible to lead a life of freedom from fear, worry, anger and stress. It helps in attaining physical vitality, emotional strength and stability, harmony in relationships, financial freedom and spiritual progress.

At Tej Gyan Foundation, Sirshree imparts this understanding through a System for Wisdom – a series of retreats that guides participants step by step towards realizing the true Self, being established in the experience of self-realization, and expressing its qualities. This system for wisdom has been accredited with the ISO 9001:2015 certification.

Maha Aasmani Param Gyan Shivir

"**Maha Aasmani Param Gyan Shivir**" is the flagship Self-realization retreat offered by Tej Gyan Foundation. The retreat is conducted in Hindi. The teachings of the retreat are non-denominational (secular).

This residential retreat is held for 3 to 5 days at the foundation's MaNaN Ashram amidst the glory of the mountains and the pristine beauty of nature. The Ashram is located at the outskirts of the city of Pune in India, and is well connected by air, road and rail. The retreat is also held at other centres of Tej Gyan Foundation across the world.

You can participate in this retreat to attain ageless wisdom through a unique System for Wisdom so that you can:

- Discover "Who am I" through direct experience.

- Learn to abide in pure consciousness while functioning in the world, allowing the qualities of consciousness like peace, love, joy, compassion, abundance and creativity to manifest.

- Acquire simple tools to use in everyday life, which help quiet the chattering mind.

- Get practical techniques to be in the present and connect to the source of all answers within (the inner guru).

- Discover missing links in the practices of Meditation (*Dhyana*), Action (*Karma*), Wisdom (*Gyana*) and Devotion (*Bhakti*).

- Understand the nature of your body-mind mechanism to attain freedom form its tendencies.

- Learn practical methods to shift from mind-centered living to consciousness-centered living.

A Mini-retreat is also conducted, especially for teenagers (14 to 16 years of age) during summer and winter vacations.

To register for retreats, visit www.tejgyan.org,

contact (+91) 9921008060, or email mail@tejgyan.com

Now you can register online for the following retreats

Maha Aasmani Param Gyan Shivir
(5 Days Residential Retreat in Hindi)

Mini Maha Aasmani Shivir
3 Days (Residential) Retreat for Teens

🔍 www.tejgyan.org

Books can be delivered at your doorstep by registered post or courier. You can request the same through postal money order or pay by VPP. Please send the money order to either of the following two addresses:

WOW Publishings Pvt. Ltd.

1. Registered Office: E-4, Vaibhav Nagar, Near Tapovan Mandir, Pimpri, Pune - 411017.

2. Post Box No. 36, Pimpri Colony Post Office, Pimpri, Pune - 411017

Phone No: (+91) 9011013210 / 9623457873

You can also order your copy at the online store:
www.gethappythoughts.org

*Free Shipping plus 10% Discount on purchases above Rs. 500/-

About Tej Gyan Foundation

Tej Gyan Foundation (TGF) was established with the mission of creating a highly evolved society through all-round development of every individual that transforms all the facets of their lives. It is a non-profit organization, founded on the teachings of Sirshree.

The Foundation has received the ISO certification (ISO 9001:2015) for its system of imparting wisdom. It has centres all across India as well as in other countries. The motto of Tej Gyan Foundation is 'Happy Thoughts'.

At the core of the philosophy of Tejgyan is the Power of Acceptance. Acceptance has profound meaning and is at the core of our Being. It is Acceptance that brings forth true love, joy and peace.

Symbol of Acceptance

The Symbol of Acceptance – shown above – is a representation of this truth. The symbol represents brackets. Whatever occurs in life falls within these brackets that signify acceptance of whatever *is*. Hence, this symbol forms the centerpiece of the Foundation's MaNaN Ashram.

The Foundation is creating a highly evolved society through:

- Tejgyan Programs (Retreats, YouTube Webcasts)
- Tejgyan Books and Apps
- Tejgyan Projects (Value education, Women empowerment, Peace initiatives)

The Foundation undertakes projects to elevate the level of consciousness among students, youth, women, senior citizens, teachers, doctors, leaders, professionals, corporate and Government organizations, police force, prisoners etc.

For further details contact:

Tejgyan Global Foundation
Registered Office:
Happy Thoughts Building, Vikrant Complex, Near Tapovan Mandir, Pimpri, Pune 411017, Maharashtra, India.
Contact No: 020-27411240, 27412576
Email: mail@tejgyan.com

MaNaN Ashram:
Survey No. 43, Sanas Nagar, Nandoshi gaon, Kirkatwadi Phata, Sinhagad Road, Tal. Haveli, Dist. Pune 411024, Maharashtra, India.
Contact No: 992100 8060.

Hyderabad: 9885558100, **Bangalore:** 9880412588,
Delhi : 9891059875, **Nashik:** 9326967980, **Mumbai:** 9373440985

For accessing our unique 'System for Wisdom' from self-help to self-realization, please follow us on:

	Website Online Shopping/ Blog	www.tejgyan.org www.gethappythoughts.org
YouTube	Video Channel	www.youtube.com/tejgyan For Q&A videos: http://goo.gl/YA81DQ
facebook	Social networking	www.facebook.com/tejgyan
twitter	Social networking	www.twitter.com/sirshree
	Internet Radio	http://www.tejgyan.org/ internetradio.aspx

Pray for World Peace along with thousands of others every day at 09:09am and 09:09pm

Divine Light of Love, Bliss and Peace is Showering;
The Golden Light of Higher Consciousness is Rising;
All negativity on Earth is Dissolving;
Everyone is in Peace and Blissfully Shining;
O God, Gratitude for Everything!

www.ingramcontent.com/pod-product-compliance
Lightning Source LLC
LaVergne TN
LVHW041544070526
838199LV00046B/1821